GURKHAS

SANDRO TUCCI

GURKHAS

HAMISH HAMILTON · LONDON

First published in Great Britain 1985
by Hamish Hamilton Ltd
Garden House 57–59 Long Acre London WC2E 9JZ

Text copyright © 1985 by J. P. Cross
Photographs copyright © 1985 by Sandro Tucci

Book design by Gerald Cinamon

British Library Cataloguing in Publication Data

Tucci, Sandro
Gurkhas.
1. Great Britain, *Army*—History   2. Gurkha
soldiers—History
I. Title
355.3′1′0941   UA853.N35

ISBN 0–241–11690–2

Typeset by MS Filmsetting Ltd, Frome, Somerset
Printed and bound in Italy by
Amilcare Pizzi s.p.a., Milan

FOREWORD BY HRH, THE PRINCE OF WALES

This book by Sandro Tucci, a photographer of international standing, is a pictorial account of the life of the Gurkha soldier, from cradle to grave. The introduction is by Lieutenant Colonel John Cross who has served with Gurkhas for many years and who knows them, their country and their language intimately.

The very name 'Gurkha' is a byword for courage and steadfastness, but quite why the Gurkha soldier possesses these qualities in such abundance is perhaps less widely appreciated—this book sheds light on the matter. Nepal, his native land, is stupendously beautiful, but it can also be cruel, capable of inflicting hardship and deprivation on its inhabitants in the form of natural disasters, such as landslides and crop failures. The Gurkha's resultant spartan upbringing in a harsh environment (where survival to adulthood is in itself an achievement), his strong sense of loyalty fostered by the bonds of family, village and tribe, his stoicism in adversity and his innate cheerfulness give him so many of the characteristics of the natural soldier. They also help explain the basis of his fearsome reputation in battle.

The book also indicates why the Gurkha so readily chooses to leave his home in the Hills and become a 'lahure'—to 'go for a soldier'. There are of course economic pressures in an over-populated land, but the Gurkha soldier is in no sense a mercenary. He lives in a free country which has always been proudly independent. This spirit of independence leads him to choose soldiering as an honourable profession, entered into freely. It leads him also to stand by his oath of allegiance, freely given. It is not by chance that Nepal is Britain's oldest ally in Asia. To be associated in some way with the Gurkhas, as Colonel-in-Chief of 2nd King Edward VII's Own Goorkhas, is one of the greatest privileges of my life, as well as being one of the greatest pleasures.

'The Gurkhas are proud sons of a blessed land, where the mountains and the flowers, the rivers and the scents, all seem to talk an eternal language of beauty and peace. They are also sons of a world where nothing comes about without the pain of hard work and hungry days. Often at night I listened to the stories of the old men, talking about the hurts and fears of leaving their homes and their families to go in search of a better life in remote unknown lands. And then I remembered the tales my parents told of southern Italy, of our villages without men, of the long and lonely wait of our mothers for their long-lost sons, and everything somehow seemed to acquire a new meaning. There was a mystery; it had been unveiled, and become a fact of life.

'One day, at a British Gurkha centre, I met a boy who had walked for thirteen days, alone, to go to the mythical British Army. He came from Rukum, in the west of Nepal, he had no clothes other than what he was wearing, he knew nothing about anything, except maybe how to tend his sheep or collect wood and water. Still he smiled, with the strange gentleness of the Hill people.

'To him, whether he was recruited or not, to the people of Nepal, to the British officers who give such a remarkable example of fairness, dedication and love to their "men", this book is intended as a small tribute.'

SANDRO TUCCI

ACKNOWLEDGEMENTS: First and foremost I must thank His Royal Highness The Prince of Wales for his most generous Foreword to this book.

I must also thank John Cross for his marvellously detailed introduction to the world of the Gurkhas, written with such a loving eye. I would like to express my most sincere gratitude to the British Army, and in particular to the Gurkha Brigade for the help, assistance and splendid hospitality given to me while taking the photographs in this book. Thanks are due too to Lincoln Potter for taking the pictures on pages 144–7, when I was unable to make the journey, and to Sunil Sethi for his editorial help.

Lastly, I would like to give thanks to the Nepalese officers and soldiers of the Brigade for having always graciously and gently understood what I was trying to do, and for having taken care of me in such a wonderful way. My activities may have seemed to them so inconsequential and so little important, but, if they did, they never said so.

INTRODUCTION BY J. P. CROSS

Nepal: the name conjures a mysterious land of sunlit valleys and swift rivers at the foot of the towering snow-capped ramparts of the Himalaya range. Precipitous hillsides, endless vistas of terraced paddy fields, shrines dedicated to myriad deities, and a smiling resilient people: these are some of the images that cross the mind's eye at a momentary invocation of this magical mountain kingdom. All these, and one more. This is the image of the invincible soldier.

Long has the name of the Gurkha been synonymous in military folklore with the red badge of courage and unflinching loyalty; long also has this body of diminutive but fierce combat warriors been the subject of rampant glorification and myth-making. And their origins are so often shrouded in conjecture that, like the mists that wreath the mountains of their land, their extraordinary saga also remains cloaked in uncertainty.

Who are the Gurkhas and where in Nepal do they come from? What are the qualities which make them among the finest soldiers in the world, a force so unique that, in this day and age, they continue to serve as fully integrated and greatly honoured members of the armies of two foreign powers, Britain and India?

To learn about these men, or to capture the essence of their fighting spirit, is at once to penetrate the mystery of their country and to chronicle the story of basic human endeavour. It is also to pay tribute to the forces of nature they spring from, to the gruelling transformation they undergo in the hands of other men; and, ultimately, to the indomitable human will for survival.

It is the Gurkha's built-in capacity to survive that sets him apart from other soldiers drawn from ethnic groups in any other part of the world. His early life, in the harsh climate and rough terrain of Nepal's treacherous mountain slopes, is a long and ardous battle against nature.

Growing up in one of the village homes—a smattering of terracotta-coloured flint dwellings that hang precariously along the ridges of the Himalayan foothills—a Gurkha's childhood can be tough. Here, along the steep and stony paths savaged by chilly winds, rosy-cheeked youngsters inadequately huddled in a few rags can be seen tending a straggling herd of sheep or staggering uphill under a heavy load. They may appear an easy-going, cheerful crowd, but a closer view will reveal cracked grimy feet and shivering underfed bodies, telling of an inherent hardiness and self-reliance.

At heights up to 8000 feet above sea level these children subsist on grazing cattle and carrying water daily from deep gorges that cut into the valleys—activities that take several hours a day between classes at the local school (which is another trek of two more hours either way).

Food—that is the first essential. Firewood and water are the next. After that comes the desperate need for protection against illness. Hospitals are rare. Sometimes a Nepali, clutching a dying baby or a fatally injured member of the clan, walks days and nights to the closest available medical centre. At the British hospital at Dharan Gurkha centre, in south-eastern Nepal, the compound is filled once a week with ailing Nepalis of all ages, who have journeyed for days to seek a cure; quickly the hospital staff go through the crowd, separating the possible survivors from those who will not recover. But there may be no more than a few beds available for the expectant crowd. In some areas of Nepal, infant mortality can be on a scale difficult to imagine in the civilized West.

But deprivation, hardship and grinding poverty do not rob the Gurkha of the finest strains of his character; his optimism, his openness and, above all, his abiding pride in his roots and identity remain untarnished by facts of birth and change. He remains to the end a Gurkha: proud, tough, resourceful.

The original definition of a Gurkha, literally meaning 'defender of cows', was a man of Mongolian stock from the ancient principality of Gurkha about fifty miles to the west of Kathmandu, whose ruler, Prithwi Narain Shah, founded modern Nepal in 1768. Now however, 'Gurkha' means any of the martial classes of Nepal, particularly those who have been recruited.

Thick-set and stocky, of an average height of about 5′ 4″, with an olive complexion, almond eyes, high cheekbones, the Gurkha has little body hair and powerful thigh and calf muscles developed from an early age by carrying heavy loads up steep hillsides. His strengths lie in this enormous stamina, physical and psychological; a predominant sense of organizational loyalty, and keen team spirit, are backed by a gritty, sinewy physique.

In social or religious terms, the Gurkha hierarchy is hard to define, if only because the martial tribes are an admixture of religions. Many Gurkhas are practising Hindus with a strong undercurrent of animism. Some are Buddhists. All believe unequivocally in a concept of destiny that is inescapable and unchangeable.

Socially the Gurkhas subscribe to conservative rituals: marriages are arranged by family elders, and sons are coveted as heirs for reasons both economic and religious. As a whole they exist peacably, though rivalries between tribes very occasionally erupt.

There are martial tribes both east and west of Kathmandu. To the east the Limbu Rai, Tamang and Sunwar tribes all speak distinct dialects. Martial tribes to the west of the capital are five: Thakur, Gurung, Magar, Pun and Tamang. Chhetris are found all over the country.

In some areas tribes of both Mongolian and Aryan extract co-exist, sometimes admittedly in uncertain harmony. But their ability to do so rests on their willing absorption of common values: physical hardship and deprivation are vital shared bonds. In the evening, as the mists envelop the surrounding landscape and the smell of woodsmoke and dung rises to the silent mountain peaks, young boys will listen to their elders talking about 'service', 'promotion' and 'pension' and stories of heroic battles fought and won, far-off places with strange sounding names and bravery awards.

These words fill an adolescent's head with dreams of unfulfilled ardour and incipient valour. He has learnt that the second victory in life—after the dogged years of keeping body and soul together—is to compete for the one job that will not only earn him a decent pension but also guarantee a position in the clan's posterity.

It is at this point that the callow Nepali youth wonders how he may become a Gurkha soldier. What indeed are the historical, geographical and social factors that transform a tough but illiterate peasant tending a few acres of terraced paddy into a powerful, highly skilled and tightly organized human machine in modern warfare?

To understand this, it is necessary to turn the clock back nearly two hundred years.

I am very proud of being a Gurkha, although my childhood years were so tough I asked myself on more than one occasion why I'd been born. I live in a small village on a steep slope that has a rhododendron forest on the top. In early spring, with the red blooms, the white snows and the blue sky it is very beautiful, not that I was really aware of it for much of the time, if only because it was part of the scenery I grew up with.

I don't know why I started mentioning the scenery when, as children, we were all too busy to notice much. Life was one long, hungry struggle. One of my earliest recollections is wondering which sort of leaf mother had told me to collect in my little back-basket to make some soup for the evening meal. There was nothing to eat in the house except a bit of flour. I didn't want to waste time so I collected as much as I could, of all sorts, and took it back. Mother had to wash and boil it all very carefully, as part of what I had collected was bitter to the taste and could have harmed us if we'd eaten it raw. Mother helped us with titbits of extra food when she could but father was always ravenous. He was kept very busy, except during the winter months when there was less to do. There was the ploughing, the sowing, the transplanting of the rice from the seed beds, the weeding, the harvesting, the threshing, the carrying, the storing of the rice—not that we had much of our own, but father helped out others, otherwise he could never have made both ends meet. Then there was a maize crop. That was all on the terraces near the village. Before the flood waters of the big river washed away what little land we had in the valley we would have to go down to work on it. It would take over an hour to get there and a bit longer than that to climb back. There were also all the other jobs to be done.

I remember herding the few goats and the two oxen. This took me up on the mountain and it was always a job to stop them from wandering too far. During the monsoon there were the leeches to contend with but there was enough greenery not to have to go too far away. In the dry season it could be fun if there was another flock to go with and we boys could play together, tipcat, hopscotch or a kind of marbles. Alone it was boring and frightening. When it wasn't a question of herding I had to search for green stuff for the buffalo. This involved a lot of clambering up over the more rugged parts of the slopes; there was always the risk of slipping down the precipice or falling off the trees. There were plenty of stories about men and boys who had been killed or maimed looking for fodder. But the buffalo had to be fed.

And if it wasn't that it was looking for firewood or helping carry water. And if it wasn't that it would be something else, always something else. I'd be dog-tired by evening and up before dawn to start all over again. And always hungry. I used to weep. But I'm running away with myself. I'd like to tell you what I've learnt about my country since I grew up. I only really understood as much as I do about it since I returned for my first leave from overseas. I'd taken it all for granted before then.

In the latter part of the eighteenth century two strong forces were moving towards one another. In India the East India Company was expanding its territories, and in Nepal, emerging from the principality of Gorkha, Prithwi Narain Shah was also bent on expanding his domains. In those days the valley of Kathmandu was divided into three separate kingdoms: Kathmandu, Patan and Bhatgaon. The name Nepal only referred to the valley, the rest of the country was simply 'The Hills'. After a lengthy and somewhat desultory compaign, Prithwi Narain Shah completed the conquest of the valley in 1768. The previous year the East India Company had written to London on the possibilities of trade with Nepal. Also in 1767, a Captain Knox had led a force of East India Company men into Nepal at the request of the King of Kathmandu. In the event Knox did not get very far. However, the very fact that foreigners had even set foot inside Nepal was a significant disturbance of the status quo.

In 1792 General Amarsing Thapa, uncle of the King who had replaced Prithwi Narain Shah on the latter's death, made ready to march westwards to Kashmir, with a view to extending Nepal's border. But he was frustrated by the Lion of the Punjab, Ranjit Singh, who did not want to antagonize the British, and when, the same year, Nepal's eastward expansion caused a war with Tibet and soon forced a withdrawal, the Gorkhas found themselves thwarted on both flanks. (It was in this year that a Treaty of Commerce and Friendship was proposed between Britain and Nepal, though this was not signed until 1801.)

The British, not wishing to antagonize China over the status of countries between their two spheres of influence, preferred to have a buffer region rather than fixed mutual borders. This policy resulted in the British keeping further south than they might have done in parts of Kashmir, in Nepal, Sikkim, Bhutan and the North Eastern Frontier Agency in north Assam. This arrangement kept Nepal independent, but its legacy has soured modern Sino-Indian relationships. At the time, however, the Gorkha rulers preferred to believe the evidence of the own eyes and were fearful of British designs. They refused to accede to the British request for diplomatic ties.

By 1812 the kingdom of Nepal was bigger than it is today, stretching from the Kashmir border in the west to Bhutan in the east. The Gorkhas sought help against the British from the Chinese, but received an evasive reply. Nevertheless, the Gorkhas were still determined to expand and the British were equally determined to prevent them. A clash, sooner or later, was inevitable.

The war started in September 1814, over a few small possessions in the central Terai. The British had an army of 21,000, the Gorkhas of 16,000. There were two bloody campaigns that ended in 1815 with the Treaty of Segauli, which was ratified in March 1816. During the military operations the British forces were clumsy and suffered from senescent generalship. The net result was that inherent Gorkha stubbornness in adversity and the competence of the Gorkha general counteracted much of the superiority of the East India Company's troops; the fighting proved a great deal harder than the British had expected. This was the first occasion on which the British were impressed by the fighting spirit and other qualities of the Gorkhas—and they were, greatly impressed. A Scotsman called James Baillie Fraser, who served in these campaigns, wrote of the Gorkhas that 'they fought us in fair conflict like men and, in the intervals of actual combat, showed us a courtesy worthy of a more enlightened people'. To some starving Gorkhas in a beseiged fort he paid this tribute: 'they would die in their trenches, hopeless for success, for the sake of honour and the debt of salt'.

Small wonder that these people excited, and still do excite, the admiration of the British who, seeing such brave conduct in the 1814–15 war, parleyed with them and incorporated them as four new battalions in the service of 'John Company', as the East India Company was known (hence, in all probability, the universal nickname of 'Johnny Gurkha'). This happened immediately in the wake of one particularly fierce engagement in which General Amarsing Thapa was defeated: the Gorkha troops lay open to the mercy of the East India Company's forces but, instead of reprisals, the impressed British commanders offered to Amarsing's men service in the Company, which was accepted then and there. The British withdrew and, in the eyes of those in Kathmandu, the danger of foreign intervention receded.

Units later known as the 1st, 2nd and 3rd Gurkha Rifles, with one other that was later disbanded, were formed on 24 April 1815. These regiments are still in being as the 1st and 3rd Gorkha Rifles of the Indian Army and the 2nd King Edward VII's Own Goorkhas (The Sirmoor Rifles) of the British Army.

Despite the steps taken to end the fighting, the war continued when the Gorkha Government failed to abide by the provisions of the Treaty of Segauli. The British planned another invasion of Nepal in 1816. But in the event the Gorkhas sued for peace before it took place and the treaty was ratified.

The first major and searching test of Anglo-Nepalese relations was made in 1857, at the time of the Indian Mutiny. In 1846 the Maharaja of Nepal, Jangabahadur Rana, had done something hitherto unthinkable. He had defied some basic tenets of the Hindu faith and made a journey 'over the black water' to Britain, where he had met Queen Victoria. He had been most impressed with all he has seen. When the Indian Mutiny broke out eleven years later, not only did all Gurkha units stand by their oath of loyalty to the British, unlike most of their Indian counterparts, but the Maharaja himself led a column of Nepalese Army troops down into India for the defence of British interests. He returned with considerable prestige and booty, both in concert with the times.

At Delhi the 2nd Goorkhas fought alongside the 60th Rifles (now the 2nd Royal Greenjackets). They suffered 327 casualties, including eight of their nine British officers, out of a strength of 490. But for this tenacity of purpose under appalling conditions—they repulsed twenty-six major attacks when the weather was at its worst—the British position in India could have been more tenuous than it already was.

In recognition of their outstanding services and of the fact that they were the first 'Native Infantry Regiment' to fight alongside the British, the Governor-General in Council granted the regiment the exceptional honour of a third colour. In 1858, the 60th Rifles, with whom a close association had been formed which still exists to this day, petitioned that the 2nd Goorkhas should be allowed to 'conform their dress to that of the 60th and that their sepoys should in future be known as riflemen'. Furthermore, at the command of Queen Victoria, a 'truncheon', to be carried by the regiment as a unique and special mark of recognition of their outstanding devotion and gallantry at Delhi, was presented. Almost a hundred years later at the time of the coronation in 1953, Queen Elizabeth II commanded that the truncheon be suitably inscribed to record that it had been carried in the coronation procession.

The system of denoting regiments in the early days varied greatly and often. Some units with Gurkhas in them were named, others numbered. By 1902 there were ten regiments, numbered 1 to 10, with two battalions each. The battalion number is written first, the regimental number second, so, in short, the 'First Battalion of the Second Gurkha Rifles' is written as '1/2 GR' and the 'Second Battalion of the Tenth Gurkha Rifles' is written as '2/10 GR'. An 11th Gurkha Rifles was in being from 1917 to 1920. Collectively all the Gurkha units were known as the 'Gurkha Brigade'.

Even before the Gurkha connection, men had gone to Lahore in India to enlist in the army of Ranjit Singh, thus earning the name of 'lahure' which is still in current use. After the East India Company link, regiments set up their own recruiting arrangements individually. Recruiting was not centralized until much later. It must not be imagined that Nepal's rulers were always happy to see recruiting outside Nepal continuing; indeed, during one spell, the punishment for going to join the Indian Army was death. This resulted in men who had somehow managed to slip through not returning home when granted leave. They stayed in India, often marrying locally and establishing colonies of Gurkhas in a number of places.

From the time of the Indian Mutiny until World War I the Gurkhas saw active service in Burma, Afghanistan, the North-East and North-West Frontiers of India, Malaya, Malta, Cyprus, Tibet and China. In the First World War 200,000 Gurkhas volunteered for service. With over 20,000 casualties they fought, were wounded and died in France and Flanders, Mesopotamia, Persia, Egypt and the Suez Canal, Gallipoli, Palestine and from Salonika to the strife-torn Russo-Turkish frontier area. Britain's supreme aware for gallantry, the Victoria Cross, was extended to Gurkhas and Indians in 1911 and during this war was twice awarded to Gurkhas, in 1915 in France and in 1918 in Egypt.

In 1919, as a result of the help Nepal had given during the war, Britain gave that country a million rupees annually.

After the war Gurkhas saw active service in the Third Afghan War and in campaigns on the North-West Frontier of India, particularly in Waziristan. Then, in 1923, a Treaty of Perpetual Peace and Friendship was signed between Britain and Nepal, which superseded the Treaty of Segauli.

In World War II, there were no fewer than forty Gurkha infantry battalions with, in addition, parachute, training, garrison and porter units and eight major units from the Nepalese Army. Side by side with British and Commonwealth troops, the Gurkhas fought from Syria through the Western desert in North Africa to Italy and Greece, from north Malaya to Singapore and up through Burma to Imphal, then forward again to Rangoon. In this war casualties exceeded 23,000, with 7544 men losing their lives. A further ten Victoria Crosses were won by Gurkhas: one in Tunisia, two in Italy and seven in Burma.

Trouble in Palestine, after the war, in the Dutch East Indies, French Indo-China, Burma and the blood-letting which led up to the troubled division of the sub-continent into an independent India and Pakistan all called for the involvement and the lives of Gurkhas. Up until that time no Gurkha had served under Indian officers: Gurkhas had always been welcome in British soldiers' canteens, Indian soldiers never. Memories of the mutiny died very hard.

Indian independence had for many years not been seriously in doubt. What had been, though, was when and how. In the event it took place sooner than expected by the British, but during the painful and protracted negotiations at the very top echelons of government the future of the Gurkha Brigade was a small but important point. Very delicate negotiations were conducted between the government of Britain, Nepal and India, and a division of the Gurkha Brigade between the armies of Britain and India was eventually agreed upon.

It was, in fact, entirely due to the last Viceroy of India, Lord Mountbatten, that Gurkhas were included in the British Army. In 1947, while in Delhi, the Prime Minister of the United Kingdom, Clement Attlee, had sought Mountbatten's advice on the possibility of transferring some Gurkha regiments to the British Army. Mountbatten's answer was that there had been twenty-three battalions of Gurkhas under his command during the war—when he had been the supremo of South-East Asia Command—and that they were the best battalions he had had. Britain would be most ill-advised to lose the services of such magnificent, cost-effective and efficient soldiers. It seems likely that if there had not been someone of Lord Mountbatten's stature to champion the Gurkha cause at this stage, then the Brigade of Gurkhas in its present form might never have come into being. It should not be thought that this unique inclusion of non-British troops into the British Army was entirely popular either in Nepal of Britain, to say nothing of India's feelings.

From that point, negotiations were initiated which resulted in permission to continue recruiting Nepalese citizens of the traditional martial classes into the British and Indian Armies, who were to be regarded, at the insistence of the Nepalese Government, as fully integrated members of those armies. Such was the need for secrecy over these delicate negotiations that all Gurkha units were kept in the dark about them. The situation was a particularly sensitive one since Gurkhas troops were available for the dreadful task of suppressing riots and escorting the countless floods of refugees between India and Pakistan which the widespread, unceasing communal strife had unleashed as well as causing the deaths of millions.

The upheaval was quite devastating, and that discipline held as it did, before partition in the entire Indian Army and after it in the Gurkha Brigade, belied much anti-British propaganda. In addition, that the Gurkhas' role was something everybody took for granted was an accolade of its own.

Independence had been fixed for 15 August 1947. Suddenly, with no preliminary warning, on 8 August, a signal was sent to all Gurkha units announcing that, of the ten regiments, the 2nd, 6th, 7th and 10th Gurkha Rifles had been selected for service in the British Army, the remainder to stay in the Indian Army. Almost at once came another signal, setting out, in outline only, the Terms and Conditions of Service for the British Army. There was only until 15 August for soldiers of every regiment to make up their minds whether or not to accept them. To expect the soldiers to decide their future so quickly and with the scant details available was unrealistic. Morale was not high in any case. All units had lost many British officers on demobilization; many Gurkhas had not been home on leave for years; and at no time before had any Gurkha even been asked to serve permanently overseas. This would be an added and unknown dimension to the future pattern of events.

It was against this background that the Gurkhas were asked what they wanted as regards their future. As soon as the decision to have Gurkhas in the British Army had been made known in August, a referendum—known as the 'opt'—had been held for all Gurkhas in all ten regiments to determine their individual wishes. They were all given the choice of whether they wanted to stay with their regiments or move to the other army. In the event another 'opt' was held towards the end of 1947, men in regiments staying with the Indian Army no longer being given the option of joining the British Army.

For men in the four regiments chosen for Britain there were three choices: to stay in their units, that is to say, join the British Army, to transfer to a unit staying with the Indian Army, or to go home on discharge or pension. Full details of the Terms and Conditions of Service were by then known, but since the previous August the cumulative effect of organized anti-British propaganda and pressure applied by Indian sympathizers put the Gurkhas under tremendous strain.

The nearer a unit was stationed to Delhi, the fewer men opted for service in the British Army. For the remaining British officers themselves, the period was one of horror, confusion and sickness at heart at their being unable to stand by their men in a world which, it must have seemed to the Gurkhas, had gone mad.

It had been a matter of great concern to both officers and men as to which regiments would be chosen to serve Britain. It was felt that regiments with 'titles' would be picked so that continuity of proven connections with the crown would be retained. Into this category fell the 1st King George V's Own Gurkha Rifles (The Malaun Regiment), the 2nd King Edward VII's Own Gurkha Rifles (The Sirmoor Rifles), the 3rd Queen Alexandra's Own Gurkha Rifles, the 4th Prince of Wales' Own Gurkha Rifles and the 5th Royal Gurkha Rifles (Frontier Force). Eight of the ten regiments were composed of westerners and only the other two, the most recent additions to the Gurkha Brigade (7 GR and 10 GR), were recruited from the east of Nepal.

However, there was in the end an equal east-west split. This decision was heavily influenced by three of the regiments having one battalion each in Rangoon, Burma, so it was cheaper and quicker to take them from there to their new homes in Malaya, Singapore and Hong Kong. With their historical connections with the British Army, the 2nd Goorkhas—as they still call themselves—were the obvious choice as the fourth regiment. The other battalions, regimental centres and the embryo headquarters were also in India or Pakistan at the time of partition.

For those units coming over to the British Army there were many problems to be solved, all against a background of turbulence and a shortage of time for proper planning. Each man had to be re-enlisted and sworn in, and a completely new system of documentation and accounting had to be opened. Clerks, being the most susceptible to Indian propaganda, were among the heaviest casualties, so the difficulties of proper preparation were exacerbated considerably. Many recruits were wanted as no battalion was up to strength; indeed, two had fewer than a hundred men. Conditions in the recruiting depots were strained and hectic: quality had to be sacrificed for quantity.

As operations demanded more and more soldiers, so the call to use recruits under training became overwhelming. Before they had learnt how to fire their rifles they were sent to guard key points and sometimes even on operations. Their orders for operational guard duties were 'to refrain from loading their rifles but to use the kukri or bayonet instead'. This lack of basic training was never properly made good and those early recruits lost out badly towards the end of their service.

The Malayan emergency and later the confrontation in Borneo, as the two campaigns were officially known, were two purely guerrilla campaigns. The first involved an elusive enemy, seldom seen or brought to action, but constantly sought and harried under testing conditions. The second was fought against an enemy that was well-equipped, aggressive and ready to fight it out.

The Malayan campaign, like that in Borneo, was conducted in support of an established government. The two major differences were that in the former the insurgents rarely took any offensive action after 1949, but the Indonesians never let up; and in the latter cross-border operations were undertaken. Although both campaigns were directed by the high command, the initiative, resourcefulness and self-reliance in remote situations of the man on the ground counted for far more than had been the case during the Burma war. It was the soldiers who slogged it out, bearing the brunt of all the unpleasantness, despite the fact that their British and Gurkha officers of up to company level were also operating in the jungle. The Gurkhas' jungle skills, their patience in patrolling and ambushing and their fierceness in combat and sustained courage, especially in the early days of the emergency, came in the nick of time to save Malaya.

At the first investiture to be held in Kuala Lumpur in 1950, the Brigade of Gurkhas, who were only about one quarter of the security forces, accounted for thirty-seven out of fifty-one awards.

One of the recipients was a lieutenant (King's Gurkha Officer) Ganesh Gurung of 1/2 GR who, with sixteen men—including those whose recruit training had been seriously interrupted—met an occupied enemy camp. The Gurkhas were outnumbered. They moved up to the camp stealthily and at about twenty-five yards saw a sentry armed with a tommy gun about to engage them. Ganesh, only armed with a pistol, took the rifle from the soldier next to him and shot the sentry. The sound of the shot caused another sentry to investigate and Ganesh shot him. Then an automatic weapon opened up and Ganesh, standing up so he could see his targets, had a remarkable escape when bullets went between his legs, wounding two men behind him. Despite being fired on, Ganesh saw and shot a third man. He then spotted the machine-gun and shot at it, hitting the magazine. By then, there being no ammunition left in the group, the Gurkha patrol charged the enemy, kukris drawn, throwing grenades. Another insurgent was killed before the remainder ran away. The camp was destroyed. Ganesh was awarded the Military Cross.

The first Distinguished Conduct Medal to be won by 1/10 GR was also presented at this time. Lance Corporal Sherbahadur Rai and his men were travelling by local train when it was ambushed, having been derailed in a cutting. Fire from both sides wounded four men. The Gurkhas, outnumbered, were called on to surrender by an insurgent approaching the carriage. He was shot and wounded by Sherbahadur, who killed a second insurgent. Sherbahadur then jumped down from the carriage and charged the enemy. His action inspired the wounded soldiers to follow him, but one was so badly wounded in the chest he had to be placed out of danger. The Gurkhas then charged the enemy again chasing them for a mile and a half. Because of the wounded men, Sherbahadur then called off the pursuit. He picked up the dead body of the insurgent, handed it over to the police and bandaged the wounds of his men. The citation recorded the 'highly courageous, bold action and inspiring leadership on the part of this lance-corporal which undoubtedly prevented a serious incident from becoming a major disaster'.

By mid-1951, the security forces had made such an impression on the insurgents that they changed their tactics. This was as a result both of concerted government policy at national level and of Gurkha mettle. Captain (King's Gurkha Officer) Dhanbahadur Gurung of 2/7 GR, who had already won the Military Cross and the Indian Distinguished Service Medal, was ambushed with forty men by eighty enemy, who were well camouflaged and in entrenched positions uphill from the Gurkhas. They were armed with six machine-guns and had plenty of ammunition. The Gurkhas were fired on as they were advancing in the open. A pitched battle including hand-to-hand fighting ensued, lasting for three hours, neither side giving ground to the other. Two Gurkhas were killed in the initial outburst of fire. The enemy often charged. Dhanbahadur made four charges uphill, a Gurkha being wounded each time. Ammunition was nearly finished. Dhanbahadur, refusing to take cover, walked up and down in front of his soldiers, brandishing his kukri in view of the enemy, who could hear him rallying his men. By the time reinforcements arrived, the enemy were about to overrun the position. The Gurkhas then counter-attacked with kurkris. Later it was learnt that eight enemy had been killed and ten wounded. (One young rifleman, Harkabahadur Rai, was awarded the Military Medal. An insurgent had tried to snatch his rifle and Harkabah-adur severed his arm with his kukri.) Dhanbahadur was awarded another Military Cross—the very least he deserved.

Giving examples of bravery is invidious to the many not mentioned, but one shining example, earning an immediate award of the Distinguished Conduct Medal, is that of Rifleman Narparsad Limbu of 2/10 GR. He was one of a patrol of four who, in 1953, met with a strongly fortified enemy camp, complete with bunker positions, with thirty insurgents ready to fight. The patrol commander was killed and two men wounded but Narparsad fought back. Having exhausted his ammunition, he collected more from the dead man and one of his companions and put the enemy to flight. He then hid the body of his patrol commander, dressed the wounds of one of the wounded men and then, having left him food and water, hid him in the jungle. (The other wounded man was not found until the next day as he had fallen down a ridge during the action.) At nightfall Narparsad set off, carrying all the arms of the patrol, and made his way to his platoon's base camp, which he reached at dawn, after a stiff climb. He then led a patrol back to the scene of the action and recovered the wounded and the body of the patrol commander.

In 1955, when there was a political amnesty in force, Sergeant Ramsor Rai, of 1/6 GR, with one other Gurkha, came across an occupied camp with ten insurgents. He sent his one man back for reinforcements and remained twenty yards away, observing all. It so happened that, since Ramsor had left camp, a call had come for the Gurkhas and only one man, a machine-gunner, was available. Having to comply with amnesty orders, Ramsor stood up and called on the insurgents to surrender. Instead of surrendering, the enemy opened fire and ran away. Ramsor managed to kill three of them and would undoubtedly have been in a position to have killed the lot (including the state 'Public Enemy Number One') had he not complied with the amnesty orders. This action resulted in Ramsor also winning the Distinguished Conduct Medal.

So the fighting continued, with the enemy becoming more and more elusive. Malaya was made independent on 31 August 1957. The emergency in Malaya continued officially until 1960 but, except for one battalion used on the Malaya-Thai border, the Brigade of Gurkhas was not used after 1958.

The 10th Gurkha Rifles had been titled the 10th Princess Mary's Own Gurkha Rifles in 1949. As from 1 January 1959, the two untitled regiments were granted royal titles and became known as the 6th Queen Elizabeth's Own Gurkha Rifles and the 7th Duke of Edinburgh's Own Gurkha Rifles.

A peaceful period of four years which then followed proved invaluable, as it enabled units to widen their professional horizon and train for roles other than operating against insurgents in the jungle by practising all aspects of warfare likely to be encountered in South-East Asia.

Then trouble flared up in December 1962 when a rebellion broke out in the sultanate of Brunei. 1/2 Gurkha Rifles moved in first, with other Gurkha and British battalions following on. A soldier of 2/7 Gurkha Rifles, Rifleman Nainabahadur Rai, was nominated 'Man of the Year' by the British Army for the valour he showed.

The last four of the hard-core rebels were sighted by Nainabahadur who was in overgrown rubber, a hundred yards from his nearest comrade. The rebels were first sighted at about seventy yards' range but Nainabahadur did not fire for fear of hitting his own men, some of whom were beyond the rebels and in the line of fire. The four rebels came on and the one in front saw Nainabahadur from thirty yards' range. The four charged the Gurkha who, standing by a tree in the aim position, opened fire at fifteen yards' range. His first round hit the leading rebel in the chest, passed through him and hit the second rebel in the chest. Both were killed. The other two then took cover. Nainabahadur fired another eight rounds at them, wounded and captured them both. This earned him the first of his two Military Medals.

It was this brief campaign which started the friendly links between Brunei and the Brigade of Gurkhas. Apart from specific acts of individual bravery, victory—then and always—was the result of an accumulation of the unobtrusive, steady and persistent team work at every level which occupies nearly all a soldier's time, especially on this sort of operation.

There then followed four years of continuous operations, from 1963 to 1966, against the Indonesian attempts to prevent the British colonies of Sarawak and North Borneo, later known as Sabah, being incorporated into Malaysia. The brunt of the fighting fell on Gurkha troops. This was guerrilla warfare, when the enemy struck and faded, ambushed and withdrew, terrorized then dispersed. The Gurkhas did everything that the guerrillas did, but did it better: an achievement that resulted from their inherent martial qualities, previous operational experience of jungle warfare and a very high standard of self-discipline—an unbeatable combination. The men had to live in the jungle for weeks on end, clearing an area of enemy, holding it and dominating it. Everything that the soldier needed for this was carried on his back. Ambushes were frequently used. This involved an eye for country, noting the minutest details for tell-tale signs, track discipline, marksmanship and self-discipline—no cooking, no washing with soap, often having no hot meals, making no noise and leaving behind no signs. To do otherwise meant failure. When a man is hunted for any length of time he becomes animal-like in his sharpened senses. To win a war under such circumstances, a soldier needs more of what is normally required of him, especially in country where the jungle is thicker, vaster and hillier than it had been even in Malaya and against an enemy harder than there had been during the Malayan emergency. It was even harder when the Gurkhas were engaged in cross-border operations. Without abnormal stamina, fortitude and quick reactions, and without the complete acceptance of discomfort and danger at all times, no victory would have been possible.

There was another aspect that helped victory. Gurkha soldiers were made the junior leaders of an Auxiliary Police Force, called the Border Scouts, until indigenous leaders were ready. The Border Scouts were raised from settlements along the border and were the 'eyes and ears' of the security forces. They were instrumental in preventing the Indonesians from dominating the border peoples. Without Gurkha support at a crucial time this would not have been possible to achieve.

Many acts of gallantry were performed at all levels and once more it would have been unjust to the many not mentioned had not the supreme example been the thirteenth award of the Victoria Cross made to a Gurkha, Lance Corporal Rambahadur Limbu of 2/10 GR.

His company were over the border on a feature that could only favour defence. They met the enemy who were strongly entrenched in platoon strength on top of a sheer hill, the only approach to which was along a knife-edge ridge allowing no more than three men abreast. Rambahadur, leading his support group, saw the nearest enemy in a trench, armed with a machine-gun. The enemy opened fire from ten yards, killing one Gurkha. Rambahadur charged the Indonesian, killed him and gained the trench. The fire from the whole enemy position was then directed on that trench.

Realizing that he was unable to support his platoon from this point, Rambahadur courageously left the comparative safety of his trench and, disregarding the hail of fire directed at him, returned to his support group and led them to a better position some yards ahead. He then tried to indicate his intentions to his platoon commander but, such was the noise of battle, this proved impossible. He therefore moved into the open and reported personally, despite the extreme danger of being hit both by the enemy and the other Gurkhas.

As he was reporting he saw that both men of his own group had been seriously wounded. Knowing the fearful repercussions of leaving any soldier, dead or alive, on Indonesian soil, he made three attempts to rescue them, rescuing one man at the second attempt and the second man at the third. The enemy tried all they could to prevent him. The last attempt was made in a series of short forward rushes and at one time Rambahadur was pinned down for some minutes by the intense and accurate automatic fire which could be seen striking the ground all round him. For all but a few seconds of the twenty minutes this action took, Rambahadur had been moving alone in full view of the enemy and under the continuous aimed fire of their automatic weapons. 'That he was able to achieve what he did,' wrote the *London Gazette*, quoting the citation, 'against such overwhelming odds, without being hit, is miraculous. His outstanding personal bravery, selfless conduct, complete contempt of the enemy and determination to save the lives of the men of his fire group set an incomparable example and inspired all who saw him.'

The whole battle lasted an hour, at point-blank range and with the utmost ferocity shown by both sides. At least twenty-four enemy were killed. The Gurkhas lost three killed and two wounded.

With the end of the Borneo campaign a short lull occurred before the Brigade found itself engaged in the patience-testing and generally hazardous task of keeping the peace in Hong Kong as the cultural revolution spilled over from the mainland of China. Deliberate provocation and confrontation on the part of communist China was contained by Gurkha coolness, great strength of mind and purpose, disciplined restraint and impeccable behaviour.

As a result of changing defence commitments and the reorganization of the armed forces, the decision was taken in 1966 to reduce the strength of the Brigade of Gurkhas from 14,400 to 9000, and a year later this was extended down to 6700. Compensation terms for those involved were fair, but the purchasing power of money became badly eroded with inflation soon after. In 1971, at the time of Britain's 'East of Suez' disengagement policy, British forces withdrew from Malaysia and Singapore. The Brigade of Gurkhas was redeployed in Hong Kong. By then there were only five battalions and the three corps units had been reduced in strength.

The next occasion on which Gurkha troops were used in an emergency was in 1974, when the 10th Gurkha Rifles, serving in the United Kingdom, were sent to Cyprus as a result of the deteriorating situation between the Greek and Turkish communities and the intervention from mainland Turkey. They went to the Eastern Sovereign Base Area at Dhekelia. Initially the battalion manned road blocks, searched vehicles and sent out confidence-building patrols to let the various ethnic communities see who Gurkhas were and how they operated. The men wore their traditional Gurkha felt hat rather than berets or floppy jungle hats, both to distinguish them from the other troops and to remind the Turks that these men were the descendants of those of the 5th, 6th and 10th Gurkha Rifles who had shown such bravery at Gallipoli in 1915 and of the 7th Gurkha Rifles who had showed such tenacity at Kut-al-Amara in 1916. The elder Turks remembered the Gurkhas with great respect. Everything was done to try and restore shattered confidence and to calm the fear-ridden minds of the many refugees.

The Gurkhas' aim was to safeguard the sovereignty of the base, showing complete impartiality to both communities at all times. Refugees also had to be administered. The Gurkhas were excellent in this role and had a most quietening and reassuring effect on them. In all about 25,000 people had to be catered for. Initially the work involved setting up the camp; later it was overseeing the administration. The camp run by the Gurkhas was recognized as the best organized and the happiest as well as the most efficient refugee centre on the whole island.

On a number of occasions the Gurkhas were instrumental in preventing grave situations from becoming untenable. Any sober assessment of the efficiency of the battalion's work in Cyprus has to agree that, if it had not been for the complete military competence, impartial steadfastness, untiring efforts and obvious fearlessness shown by officers and men, the Turkish Army would most certainly have occupied the major Greek Cypriot city and port of Larnaca and might well have overrun the Eastern Sovereign Base Area, with untold consequences. As it was, the 10th Gurkha Rifles was the only battalion on the island that did not actually have to engage other armies in combat.

In 1977, during Queen Elizabeth II's Silver Jubilee year, Her Majesty honoured the two senior corps units with royal titles: The Queen's Gurkha Engineers and Queen's Gurkha Signals. Prince Charles was also appointed Colonel-in-Chief of the 2nd Gurkha Rifles.

In July 1979, the first ever Gurkha contingent, men of the 6th Gurkha Rifles, went to Belize in Central America in answer to that colony's request for aid against Guatemala. Even after Belize became a sovereign nation, the commitment continued.

Apart from training for limited war, work in Hong Kong is concerned with internal security duties, assisting the Royal Hong Kong Police along the border with China and in the built-up areas of the towns.

In 1981, as a result of a reassessment of the level of army manpower which was needed to support the Hong Kong government, another Gurkha battalion was requested. This led to 2/7 Gurkha Rifles, disbanded eleven years before, being re-raised.

Duties on the Sino-Hong Kong border have become a regular feature of battalion life. The task was and still is to prevent illegal Chinese immigrants from entering the colony and to ensure stability in the border region. The bulk of such people come across the border at night, so most of the effort to catch them is during the hours of darkness, although vigilance during daylight hours is also needed. At night the standard technique is to deploy troops in three-to-four-man groups, mostly out in the open. During the winter months and the rainy season this can be very unpleasant.

These groups normally operate in conjunction with others. As the illegal immigrant has to move, the advantage lies with the military group which remains still and quiet. The group of soldiers that first sees suspects alerts the others by radio. Once the direction of movement is known, efforts are made to apprehend the illegal immigrants by surrounding them. If this is not possible a chase ensues. The normal reaction of the Chinese is to run a short distance and then hide. A search then develops. There have been some dangerous incidents during these operations that have required considerable gallantry to overcome, and Gurkha life has been lost.

After a month to six weeks on the border, the battalion reverts to other duties, normally those of a routine nature, guards and duties within the unit and outside it, as well as the task that is forever with it—training, collectively or individually, for the next eventuality. There is community relations work to occupy the battalion's time, such as building feeder roads, jetties, basketball pitches and small rural bridges, playing games with the locals, providing tannoy systems at sporting events, running youth activities and playing military music at various civic functions.

In Brunei, garrison duties and training occupy the soldiers' time and efforts, especially jungle training. There is a special team that runs courses in jungle warfare for the British Army, relying heavily on the Gurkhas for maintenance of standards. In broad terms its task is to teach a man how to live, move and fight in jungle, when the ears have to take over from the eyes for much of the time. There are many techniques involved to achieve these three basic requirements: patrolling, ambushing, river crossing, tracking, survival and many points of jungle lore, such as making bird or animal noises instead of calling by voice, disguising one's movements, estimating the age of a cut branch or a bent leaf. As a jungle warrior, the Gurkha is superb: he has infinite patience, razor-sharp eyesight, wary caution, dogged stamina, and an ability to 'read' the ground to such an extent that he has been known to track the most painstaking and elusive quarry even when the spoor has become cold. His friends and his enemies know this. The British Army would be hard pressed to maintain these skills without the Gurkhas.

Like any unit of the British Army, the Gurkha battalion in Britain is used for normal military tasks. From time to time duties include the ceremonial guarding of the monarch's residence and other important buildings. Out of political sensitivity, no Gurkha unit has been deployed in Northern Ireland.

The Gurkha battalion's camp is at Church Crookham near Aldershot in the south of England. During a two-year stint, apart from routine training and duties, the two major commitments are public duties and running the annual skill-at-arms competition at Bisley.

When the Gurkhas first appeared at the sovereign's residence and took over duties from the Brigade of Guards, they were an instant attraction, if only because they were much more than a head shorter than the Guardsmen. The Gurkhas' first glimpse of Buckingham Palace took place back in 1953, at the time of Her Majesty's coronation. A practice was held in the small hours, which involved walking the route they were later to march. As they passed the palace, the senior Gurkha officer ordered the men to walk on tiptoe so as not to waken the Queen.

In addition to the battalion in England, there are two demonstration companies for officers' and non-commissioned officers' training, and a squadron of engineers. There are also many men on courses of instruction and Her Majesty will have two senior Gurkha officers attending her as Queen's Gurkha orderly officers.

In the spring of 1982, when Argentina invaded the British possessions of South Georgia and the Falkland Islands, part of the Task Force sent by the United Kingdom Government to regain its territories was 1/7 Gurkha Rifles, then on duty in Britain. The battalion did not engage in as much action as did the other units. On one occasion when it was deployed in front of the Argentines, the invaders ran away. The reputation that the name Gurkha inspired allowed victory to be won with far fewer casualties than might otherwise have been the case.

The renown won over all these years has spread the reputation of the Gurkha as a fighting man far and wide. Their fighting record is second to none, but also combines with the myths of the kukri which is never drawn without shedding blood and may be used as a boomerang, which overlay the true facts. This mystique has credited Gurkhas with near magical powers—and the Gurkha knows that a high standard brings its own penalties of expectation. Generations of Gurkhas have upheld this reputation as they have come down from the Hills to serve the British. But service in the British Army, as much as maintaining the tradition, is also seen as the best way for a Gurkha to relieve himself, at least for a while, from the reason-deadening toil of back-breaking subsistence farming, of poverty, of debt and, dimly perceived, mental stagnation—even if death or mutilation is the price to be paid.

Between 1 January 1948 and 31 December 1982, out of 35,168 Gurkha men who served in the British Army, 247 (0.7%) were killed in action and 540 (1.54%) died of other causes – accidents, disease or very occasionally, suicide. Mental turmoil does not necessarily cease when poverty recedes.

The relationship between Britain and Nepal is unique. On 18 November 1980, at Buckingham Palace, during a state visit to Britain, His Majesty King Birendra of Nepal said: 'the people of Nepal began to admire fairness, justice, discipline and tenacity in the British character just as the British, I am sure, must have admired some inherently good disposition in the character of their Gorkha brethren. The Anglo-Nepalese encounter thus turned out to be a voyage of discovery of each other's ideals and values. This has another advantage too. It proved that Nepal rejects, totally and unequivocally, any idea of subjugation, thus stubbornly refusing to become a province of any other country. It was based on these cherished principles of non-interference, sovereign equality and unquestioned independence, that Nepal became a close friend of Great Britain.'

Proof of that close friendship is evinced in the Tripartite Agreement that stipulates that it is the Nepal Government's wish that recruitment is open to 'all martial classes'. Both in the west and in the east, up to 80,000 young men try their luck each time recruiting opens, and to reduce this number of aspirants—not all of whom are from the martial classes—to a manageable figure, means that the two recruiting centres need careful planning.

The process starts in Hong Kong, where the Record Office calculates the requirement to make up for natural losses through men retiring. A demand is passed to the British authorities in Nepal and is divided between east and west, Dharan and Pokhara, for its fulfilment.

In overall command of British Army units in Nepal is a brigadier who is also the chief recruiting officer, although the bulk of all recruiting falls on his staff in the two centres. There are two British deputies who have a team of retired but re-employed Gurkha officers and ex-non-commissioned and ex-warrant officers. The former, known as area retired officers, live in camp; the latter, known as recruiters, or locally 'Galla Walas', live at home. The two deputies are responsible for tapping the areas in the 20,000 square miles of territory for which each is responsible for the most suitable material. Recruiters in camp are then given passes, issued by the Nepalese Government and substantiated by the recruiting centres, authorizing them to bring selected lads from the Hills to the camp.

By the time I was seventeen I was a strong boy. I put that down to having spent time in the upland pastures with the herds when I was younger. After father died, mother and the others were in dire straits. Luckily an uncle took pity on me, but he was very strict. I had to go with the herds three years in succession. The journey to the pastures took several weeks because the cattle moved so slowly. We had large dogs with us to help protect the flocks from the leopards and other predators. We'd get back to the village six to eight months later. With the lush grass the cows would give enough milk for us all to have enough. I'm sure it was then I grew strong.

For as long as I could remember I'd had it in the back of my mind to join the army. The village elders would gather around and talk endlessly about the time they were lahures. They made it all sound so easy, so interesting, so manly: you are fed, clothed, paid, saw many strange places—the 'world' for most of us started the other side of the next village—and here was I, always hungry, never having worn a pair of shoes and never having worn new clothes. I knew the villagers thought I had a chance of being accepted by the Galla Wala because, after my fourteenth birthday, I was told to stop collecting fodder for the buffalo from the most dangerous places in case I slipped and ruined my chances.

One day my friend, who was a year older than me, went on his own to the British recruiting camp. It took him three days and that didn't include the bus ride down to near the Indian border to Paklihawa camp. He'd borrowed some money to do it, but when he got there he found that the system had been changed. So he had to come back. He was in a dreadful state as he had used all the money and was in debt. He couldn't see how he'd ever get any more. However, he made a deal with his creditor, who was an ex-Indian Army man. When the man next went to India to collect his pension, he would take my friend with him and try to enlist him in his old regiment by saying they were father and son. Provided that he was accepted, my friend would pay over on his first leave enough to cover the debt and the interest—that was 36% a year—plus travelling expenses and other costs. My friend had not much option and there seemed to be a good chance of success. In fact he was lucky, otherwise he'd still be heavily in debt.

I didn't want to join the Indian Army without having tried for the British Army first. I'd have to wait for the 'Galla Wala' to visit my village. This most important of men lived more than two days' walk away and there was no guarantee he'd be at home if I went to his village, so I waited, hardly daring to go far from home in case I missed him. Mother was as desperate as I was. She felt that there might be some hope of putting a new roof on the house, which was very leaky, and paying back some of father's debts, if only I could join up. By then my mother looked a really old woman, but she was still in her forties.

The 'Galla Wala' came at last. There must have been a dozen of us from our village alone and I was dismayed when he said he could only take two of us. 'Apart from the fact that that is the quota, who would do the work if I took you all?' he said. 'I've got over thirty villages to visit and I've only got to provide sixty lads for Hill Selection.' How he picked me I can only attribute to what is written on my forehead—that which the gods write at birth and the skin hides all through our lives—but he did pick me. I was told when and where to meet him: two days' walk away, five weeks later. Did I count those days?

'Hill Selection', when a two-man team of area retired officers goes to a predetermined location to eliminate all but the best candidates through various tests, is the next step. For the recruiters it is also a good safeguard against charges of nepotism or bribe-taking, as the ratio of youths ultimately chosen is six or seven to one.

A vast crowd of interested spectators always gathers at Hill Selection, hoping that their man will be among the successful. Care must be taken to choose a site that will not be swamped by spectators or broken up by rowdies, and will have enough local backing to feed the throng. By this time the recruiter will have weeded out those whose basic physical characteristics—age, height, weight, build—are obviously a bar to recruitment. At Hill Selection the measuring is reported and an assessment of each aspirant's abilities is made. It normally takes two days' hard work to select the men for the next stage.

It is very hard to tell the age of a young Gurkha, especially as he himself has no clear idea of when he was born. Birthdays have no significance in Nepalese Hill society. There was once a case of father and son being recruited in the same batch. When asked later how it had happened, the father said that he had 'shaved in hot water that morning' and that his son had stood on his toes, unnoticed by the recruiter, when he was being checked for minimum height! For the British Army, 'general duties' soldiers are taken between eighteen and twenty-one, though clerks might be as old as twenty-four.

The lucky few who pass Hill Selection are registered closely enough to ensure that a man cannot take another's place before the next stage, which takes place at the recruiting centre. Here there is a highly systematized programme for the final selection, where another fifty percent are weeded out. The processing includes physical, mental, medical, educational and stamina testing, followed by interviews conducted by the recruiting staff. Once again all the physical details are recorded. This may seem a waste of time, but strange things can happen. One youth said he was embarrassed to strip to his underpants for weighing on Hill Selection, so he was weighed in his trousers and found to be heavy enough. He again declined to take off his trousers when he was told to on inspection at the recruiting centre; eventually, under pressure he did, and was found to have several heavy stones tied to the inside of his legs which, once removed, left him sadly underweight. Another youth who knew he was underweight but had the correct chest measurements, both normal and expanded, drank five pints of water and ate eight bananas just prior to the weigh-in. So full had he stuffed himself, that although his weight was fine, he was physically unable to expand his chest more than a derisory half-inch instead of the required two. Both were rejected, although given full marks for ingenuity. If a boy were not almost always hungry and the source of his next meal always a problem, why should he want to go through such a rigmarole of deception?

One of the common, and wrong, beliefs is that only the sons of serving or retired British Army Gurkhas are accepted. Almost the reverse is true in reality, because when the formative years of a boy's life have been spent with his parents in the Army, especially if his father has been senior enough to have his family with him full-time, rather than in the Hills, the boy is, in many cases, robbed of that recognizable but undefinable quality required in all Gurkhas wanting to be recruited.

Rejection at the final selection is to the unsuccessful the kiss of death, a negation of manhood. At one time every recruit appearing for it had to have his hair cut. For a shorn man to return immediately to his village was such a crushing burden that many could not shoulder it, slipping free of the recruiter who was duty-bound to take rejected men back home and drifting into India, like a whipped cur hiding to lick his wounds.

Processing can take up to two weeks. On the morning when the results are announced the atmosphere is tense. The young men are nervous as they are assembled to be told their fate. As the names are called out, some answer with a joyful shout, running to where they are directed, otherwise there is silence. Some come forward demurely, almost in a daze, hardly believing their ears, perhaps fearful they will be pulled back even at this eleventh hour. Some openly weep for joy. Those who remain grow more and more solemn. And then it is over, the last name is called, with new lives about to be carved and old ones returning to the furrow they had hoped to escape. The rejected draw money to get them home. Some weep; others, in their heart of hearts, knew they would be unsuccessful. There are those who leave the camp, determined to return next time, now that they have experienced the processing and are the wiser for it, knowing that the interviews showed hesitation instead of confidence and the tests showed weaknesses; such men are in the majority. There are those who realize that they are not up to it and do not want to risk another rebuff. A high proportion of those who return are selected, some even on the third occasion.

The new recruits are attested at a simple ceremony when they take an oath of allegiance to Her Majesty Queen Elizabeth II. The parade is made as formal as circumstances permit, with the new soldiers trying so hard they look like mechanical toys.

Before leaving the camp on the first stage of the Gurkhas' journey to Hong Kong for basic training, tension rises, intensifying with the journey to Kathmandu, which the majority of recruits will never have seen. The night flight to Hong Kong shows dramatically the organization and administration of the 'military machine' which they have joined and the journey culminates, on arrival early the next morning, in a cultural shock of considerable magnitude.

The men's destination is the Training Depot, Brigade of Gurkhas. On arrival they are given time to acclimatize mentally and physically before they start on rigorous training which normally lasts for nine months. The aim of recruit training is to produce the lowest grade of private soldier. Training is based on the same syllabus as for British recruits with supplementary subjects to take account of the Brigade of Gurkhas' Far East role and the differences in ethnic characteristics and educational background.

The first spell of training is entirely basic and lasts for thirty-two weeks. Particular emphasis is placed on skill-at-arms with personal weapons; physical fitness, to build up the men who have lacked a decent diet; discipline; limited war and counter-revolutionary tactics at section level; and education, which provides much of the essential foundation upon which most other training depends.

This is followed by eight weeks of more advanced training that consists of instruction on platoon support weapons, an introduction to internal security—crowd control—weapons and tactics, further tactical training including field firing on open ranges, and basic radio user instruction.

The new soldier is then allocated to a regiment, selection being based on training results. This also involves a parade at which he is given his regimental cap badge before he joins his unit. If members of the recruiting staff who had enlisted him were to see him on this day, they would have much difficulty in recognizing the impeccably dressed and physically confident soldier with the gauche, uncoordinated, hesitant youth of ten months before.

The Gurkha has found himself, for the first time in his life, in a position where his activities, his training, his welfare, his comfort, his problems, his very livelihood are the concern of a dedicated band of motivated, talented individuals whose cause is service, not self-interest, and whose bedrock of faith is trust. He finds himself in a traditional but forward-looking society with a stricter code of conduct than he ever experienced before.

How does the Gurkha see his British officer? Certainly the British officer, as a type, is regarded as a quick-reacting, fair-minded, professional soldier whose breadth of vision lets him rise above all matters except 'professional integrity'. He cannot judge a man on anything but merit, efficiency, guts, behaviour, endeavour, temperament and results. It cannot matter to him who, of the traditional martial classes, comes to serve, so long as he is of the correct stock, of the correct mould and has potential; nor does it matter who gets promotion so long as it is the best man who gets it. Add to all that the knowledge embedded in tradition, if not in folklore, that the British officer is above everything except service and therefore can be implicitly trusted in all matters, from correcting examination papers to making detailed and balanced tactical plans for going into battle; and Gurkhas marvel at their officers' compassion and their sincerity.

The Gurkha sees the British, and all that a military life means, as one way of improving himself in a relationship where merit counts and trust is paramount; the British, in turn, see the Gurkha as epitomizing the type of soldier they most require. With his traditional brimmed headgear, the Gurkha felt hat, seldom slipping from its correct angle, with innate style in peace-time and enough camouflage in war, the Gurkha symbolizes the continuity of old-style values and contemporary adaptability.

Once a Gurkha has passed out of the Training Depot he can expect, under normal circumstances, to serve until he qualifies for a pension. He is signed on for four years to start with, then again at the seven, ten, twelve and fifteen-year points, and thereafter a year at a time. A man's first leave will normally be after three years' service. Many get married then. Even so, after a strenuous three-year tour, time hangs heavily on his hands. During his second leave, after six years or so, he may have saved enough money to buy some land to build himself a house, though possibly only a ground floor and a roof.

After a minimum time of fifteen years and a maximum of thirty-two, a Gurkha qualifies for a pension. As he probably joined the army when he was between eighteen and twenty years old, by the time he returns for good he is comparatively still a young man. If he has saved wisely, that money, including terminal grants, and his pension, will stand him in good stead on his return to the Hills.

The duration of a Gurkha's service can depend on his rise through the ranks. By being promoted and becoming a 'Gurkha officer'—Gurkha lieutenant, captain or major—he attains longer years in service. A Gurkha major, becomes, by dint of his seniority and commanding position, the undisputed guru of his unit. Gurkha officer ranks are unique to the Brigade of Gurkhas, as officers hold the Queen's commission although remaining junior to those commissioned at Sandhurst. Some especially well-qualified Gurkhas are commissioned exactly as their British counterparts: they undergo a full training course in the military academy at Sandhurst, and a few may further qualify for advanced staff training and command of a major unit as lieutenant-colonel.

From participating in full-scale hostilities to providing international aid, from performing in band tours to ceremonial duties, a Gurkha is, at all times, ready for any role or eventuality. Such split-second readiness is drilled into him night and day through his gruelling routine in the unit, so that his automaton-like efficiency and preparedness can trigger him into instant action. But his working life is not all monotony. The Gurkha's inherent love of music, of sport, and his devotional life, are all accommodated in Camp.

Music is an old military tradition and the Gurkha, a hillman, is a piper by nature. Back home he will fashion a flute of wood while tending his flock to keep himself company. Over the years the Scots, the hillmen of Britain, have taught Gurkhas to pipe and drum, running courses in Scotland so that the ceremonial guards, over a hundred strong, will always love pipes and drums or have, as in the case of the 2nd Gurkha Rifles, a military band and buglers. In war these men become the unit's stretcher bearers and first-aid men.

Equal attention is paid to a Gurkha's religious susceptibilities. Each major unit has a Hindu priest attached to attend to the rituals and religious rites that constitute the major events of a Hindu's life: marriage and childbirth; or the crucial moments in a child's initiation such as the ceremony of his first haircut or first meal; or the ritualistic cremation at death that is the ultimate purification of the soul in its journey to reincarnation.

Then there are the religious festivals, the most important for the Gurkha being the annual celebration of Dashera every autumn. Traditionally, this is the time when Nepalis, being a martial race, sacrifice animals, goats or buffaloes, in offering to the gods. In Gurkha units, however, the sacrifice of only one animal is permitted. The candidate chosen to commit the sacrifice is selected with great care, and in his perfect consummation of the ritual he must be able to decapitate the animal in a clean, single stroke. Dashera is followed a month later with the festival of Diwali—lamps are lit at night, fireworks fill the dark sky and brothers visit their sisters to be anointed with a 'tika' or vermillion mark upon their foreheads.

At least once during his term of service, and more often after promotion, a Gurkha soldier is allowed to have his family join him for a tenure of three years. Free education is provided for the children and accommodation for the families; in other cases, a soldier's dependants are adequately provided for by a registered charity in the UK, known as the Gurkha Dependents Fund. Up to £1600 can be received, in return for a modest annual subscription, by a Gurkha's family if he dies in service.

If not, the last years of his service are oriented to help rehabilitate him in the home he left years before as an unlettered youth of seventeen or eighteen. Resettlement courses are run in Dharan to train retiring Gurkhas tackling subjects as varied as animal husbandry to banking and rural administration. Private funding for such schemes comes from several sources; Horace Kadoorie, a well known Hong Kong philanthropist, for instance, runs a special training farm for Gurkhas in the New Territories.

A highly-decorated Gurkha captain, Lalhabadur Limbu, famous for leading a bayonet charge to dislodge a Japanese entrenchment in Burma in World War II, describes his valedictory moments in service:

I led a bayonet charge and received the reward of a Military Medal. I never asked for it but I was awarded it.

At the end of the war, during the 'opt', I had the chance of going home, but I thought I'd try and earn a pension. The regiment was chosen for the British Army. I was called in with the others and asked what I wanted to do. I said I wanted to stay on. I was told that, as I wasn't very clever, I'd stick at Naik if I went across to the British.

Fine. I'd never asked to be a Naik either. 'It's up to you,' I said. I went across to Malaya and was immediately made a sergeant. 'You've got a decoration, so you've been promoted,' said the major, 'but you won't go any higher.'

Trouble broke out and I took a platoon of men to the jungle. Had a brush with the enemy. I was awarded another decoration, not that I'd ever given it much thought. I was called into the office one day and told that, although I'd go no further, I was going to be promoted to warrant officer. So there I was, a sergeant-major!

'That's as far as you'll go,' said the major saheb, not the first one, but another. Then a third major was posted in and, quite why or how I don't know, but he recommended me for commissioning. 'You'll have to stay as Gurkha Lieutenant, but you won't mind that,' I was told.

I just said that I'd never asked to be commissioned and that I was very satisfied. I thought to myself what we say up in the Hills: 'In matters of God, Government and Games, there is neither victory or defeat, but that the Referee wills it.'

And here I am, going home on maximum Gurkha captain's pension. I was rewarded, twice, for a battle I fought. It didn't last very long in both cases. But for twenty years I've been rewarded for having been rewarded. You British are a strange lot!

Still, life can be hard for the pensioned-off Gurkha; returning to the treacherous mountainside of his birth, he suffers culture shock and the insecurity of maladjustment in his later years.

Some Gurkhas inevitably do better than others in retirement. With their worldly training in their years abroad, they find employment with international agencies operating in Nepal; some take to national politics; some manage to establish successful farms; but there are others whose difficult return to their roots is excarbated by illness and emotional insecurity and a general slide downhill.

In the first thirty-four years of its life in the British Army, the Brigade of Gurkhas had 35,168 men enlisted, of whom 19,140 were on pension as at 31 December 1982. The total strength of the Brigade represents half a percent of the population.

But whatever the end may contain, it is devoid of any trace of regret or bitterness. True to type, and years of training, the Gurkha passes away cheerfully, a smile on his lips and a salute in his heart. What sustains him in the end are the inner convictions that have made his life extraordinary: pursuit of adventure, the importance of valour, and an everlasting commitment to a code of honour.

So I consider myself very lucky. I'm a sergeant now and have a good chance of going higher. Mother is happy as she has a new house with a roof that doesn't leak, enough to eat and a young orphan to help out with the chores whom she regards as a grandson. I have a son and a daughter. We have no debts.

It's surprising how I've forgotten my earlier troubles. I never thought I would. I'm making sure my family has a good start in life. That's what it's all about. And in case I get too complacent, I sometimes think of a song my father used to sing:

> *Dashera is over, Diwali is near,*
> *The marigolds are all in bloom.*
> *On the village swing sits a maiden fair,*
> *But alas for me, there is no room.*
> *The prime of life for me is past.*
> *Long may that maiden's pleasures last.*

GURKHAS

In the mountains and valleys of Nepal: pink sunsets and white snows, but on the ground, in the villages, the struggle against the hardships of days and seasons is unremitting

The all-seeing eyes of the Nepalese gods, an emblem
of the profound religiosity of the people. One finds
them everywhere, on doors, on temples, on holy
images

One day in western Nepal I saw these two women carrying baskets full of bricks, bare-footed, up this steep mountain. All day long they carried up the slope the construction materials for a new house being built on the ridge. It was hard to tell their age, but they were not young and their faces showed all the signs of their hard life

A young girl crossing a river in west Nepal

Mustard fields in the highlands

Schools are often far from the villages they serve.
These Limbu and Rai boys from the hills of eastern
Nepal, near Hatikarka, had to walk for more than
an hour up the mountainside to reach theirs

(*Overleaf*) A young shepherd with his flock: a boy
who has grown up to be independent, self-
sufficient, capable of living alone for long periods in
a harsh habitat. He is the ideal future 'gurkha'
recruit

(*Previous page and left*) One glorious winter morning in Sikha, western Nepal, when 'hill selection' took place. Always this is a grand occasion, when retired Gurkhas, recruiting officers, relatives and local people gather to see and appraise the new batch of 'hopefuls'. Only a few will pass to the next stage. Gathered in the school yard, they take a basic education test

One inch on the chest, or a good weight, may make
all the difference

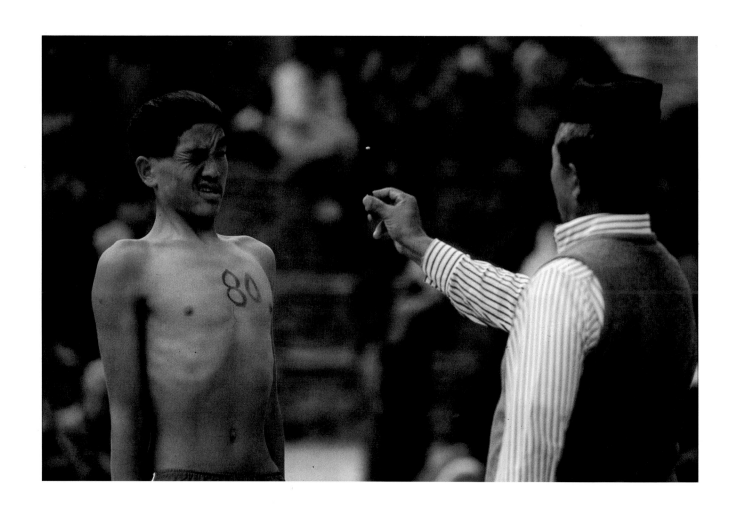

At the final selection in western Nepal this boy,
whose name I never discovered, showed up. He had
walked alone through valleys and rivers for thirteen days, from Rukum in one of the remote areas of
western Nepal. He had only the clothes he was
wearing and a letter from a British Army officer
inviting him for final selection. He was lost, almost
terrified, somehow separated from the other boys;
but he was still smiling, with gentle eyes

In the final selection, roughly one out of two prospective recruits is taken on, but *all* are determined. Going back to the village means a great loss of face both for the failed recruit and for the clan which has supported his efforts. So whether it is a tug-of-war, a five-mile run, an assault course, or an interview with the British officer, determination does not slacken

At the attestation ceremony, the freshly selected
recruits swear allegiance to the Queen

(*Right*) On the way to TDBG in Hong Kong the
recruits will stop over in Kathmandu, which most of
them will never have seen before

The day starts early: there is schooling to attend;
the uniform to be put on properly; drilling under the
eyes of NCOs who are never happy . . . until one day
the boy from the hills discovers he has become a
soldier. . . .

Soldiers must also learn how to shoot. At the yearly
shooting competition at Bisley, Gurkha units regu-
larly walk away with top honours

Boots, a kukri and a rifle—the Gurkha's essential
equipment

(*Overleaf*) Early one morning, jogging in full combat
gear. The astonished runner could only stop and
watch in disbelief

The passing-out parade, after which the recuits are posted to their respective regiments. A sergeant receives a prize cup, and the top recruit a kukri— the traditional (and domestic) Nepalese curved-bladed knife, retained by the British Army as part of the Gurkha dress

At the jungle warfare training school: learning the
techniques of river crossing

(*Previous pages*) A Gurkha patrol in the forest of Brunei

(*Left and below*) The Gurkha's adaptation to jungle conditions, his agility, his resistance to heat and humidity, make him a jungle fighter of the highest quality. In harmony with his environment, he is almost invisible

(*Overleaf*) The art of being a member of heliborne troops

(*Previous page and this page*) One of the main tasks of the Gurkha Brigade today is to secure the border between China and Hong Kong. Patrols at regular points send back young illegal immigrants almost every night

(*Overleaf*) A Gurkha unit in atomic/biological/chemical warfare gear at Church Crookham in Great Britain

(*Previous page*) New recruits are trained for riot control duties in Hong Kong

(*Left*) The assault course

(*Below*) There is a very interesting interrelation between British officers and Gurkha soldiers, which I have never seen in any other army. It is a kind of gentleness, of affection, which I guess makes war a little more bearable. I saw this brigadier, commander of the Gurkha Field Force, talking to his men during a break in training, and that moment brought this home to me

(*Previous pages*) Gurkhas on patrol and on exercise. At the end of a long war exercise, early one morning, after the 'final attack', we were all waiting for transport back to Hong Kong. The Gurkhas, who had been on exercise for almost a week, thought that a good way to spend the waiting time would be to see who could run to the top of this hill—in full combat dress—and back again the fastest. It was an amazing sight to see all these boys, tired from a long week away, running up and down the hill and enjoying every minute of it

(*Previous pages*) Gurkha pipers, impeccably uniformed, with their regimental banners flying in the wind

In Church Crookham one day I found these Gurkhas practising their bugle-playing; in the afternoon we went to a small country fair where the pipers entertained, among others, a lady with a rose

(*Overleaf*) A British officer inspecting weapons

HRH, The Prince of Wales, Colonel-in-Chief of 2nd King Edward VII's Own Goorkhas, during his visit to the Gurkha garrison on Brunei at the time of the independence celebrations

(*Overleaf*) The well-wishers waving their Union Jacks and Nepalese flags were almost blown away as the Prince of Wales's helicopter lifted off

(*Four pages on*) Hong Kong is today the Gurkha headquarters. After a two-year tour in Brunei or Great Britain, the regiment returns to Hong Kong. During Brigade of Gurkha week, this gigantic backdrop of the Crown colony provided a wonderful setting for the beating of the retreat

(*Previous pages*) HM The Queen has two Queen's Gurkha Orderly Officers. I saw Rambahadur Limbu, VC, and Dipakbahadur Gurung shortly after their investiture as QGOOs, and was full of admiration for these men who had gone so far

One of the things which struck me most about the Gurkhas in the months which I spent with them was that they always seem to be smiling

Dashera (or Dessera) is the holiest of religious experiences for the Nepalese, and in homage to the ancient ritual a sacrifice is still performed within Gurkha regiments. The stroke of the kukri must be strong and decisive to please the gods and bring their protection to the fighting men. The weapons are garlanded with flowers and blessed with the animal's blood; the men receive 'tikka' or a blessing in the centre of their foreheads which, in Hindu tradition, is the centre of the human spirit

After his term of service, which varies with his rank, a Gurkha is discharged to return to his native land. Somehow the old soldiers always remain Gurkhas, despite losing all appearance of ever having been away from Nepal. At the hill selection in Sikha I saw the retired men getting together to talk about the old times and share their opinions of the new hopefuls. Others, with money saved, will start their own business: a chicken farm, a rice farm, a restaurant with rooms to cater for tourists and passers-by

RESTAURANT MENU :-

HOT DRINKS

1. BLACK TEA
2. MILK ,,
3. MINT ,,
4. MILK COFFI
5. BLACK ,,
6. HOT CHOCOLET

BREAK & SNACKS

7. FRIED EGGS ONE
8. BOILED ,, ,,
9. SCREMBL ,, ,,
10. POCH ,, ,,
11. POTATO AMLET
12. EGGS ,, ,,
13. VEGETABLE AMLET
14. ONION ,,
15. CHEESE ,,
16. OAT PORRIGE
17. CORN ,,
18. RICE PODDING
19. PANCAKE LEMON SUGAR
20. ,, PLAIN
21. ,, /JAM
22. ,, /HONY
23. ,, /PENUT BUTTER
24. ,, /MARMALADE
25. TIBETAN
26. BREAD PLAIN
27. ,, ,, JAM
28. ,, ,, HONY
29. ,, ,, PENUT BUTTER
30. ,, ,, MARMALADE
31. CHAPATI PLAIN
32. ,, /JAM
33. ,, /HONY
34. ,, /PENUT BUTTER
35. MUESLI WITH MILK
36. ,, /CURD
37. CORN BREAD PLAIN
38. ,, ,, /JAM
39. ,, ,, /HONY
40. ,, ,, /PENUT BUTTER

LUNCH & DINNER

41. CHIEKEN SOUP
42. VEGETABLE ,,
43. TOMATO ,,
44. EGGS ,,
45. RICE DAL VEGETABAN
46. FRIED RICE ,, ,,
47. ,, ,, PLAIN
48. ,, ,, EGGS
49. ,, NOODLE VEG.
50. ,, ,, ,, EGGS
51. POTATO CHIPS
52. ROAST POTATO
53. FRIED ,,
54. BOILED ,,
55. MASAED ,,
56. POP CORN

TIBETAN

57. VEGETABLE THUKPA
58. EGGS ,,
59. MEAT ,,
60. ONION RINGS
61. SPRING ROOL
62. CUTLET CHIPS
63. SWISS ROSTLE

COLD DRINKS

64. LEMU
65. COKE
66. LEMON
67. BEER

68. XXX KHUKURI RUM
69. POKHARA RUM
70. PINEAPPLE
71. LOCAL WINE ONE

THA

On a flight to Nepal I met a Gurkha lieutenant whose father, also a Gurkha, had died at the British hospital. He was going home for the burial: as the eldest son he was to join with the priest in the performance of the necessary rites. They brought the old man to the river in a simple wooden coffin, they burnt his body, and at the last they cast his ashes on the sacred water. All was peace

157